YANKEE
DOODLE
DRUMSTICKS

OTHER YOUNG YEARLING BOOKS
BY PATRICIA REILLY GIFF YOU WILL ENJOY:

THE LINCOLN LIONS BAND

MEET THE LINCOLN LIONS BAND

THE KIDS OF THE POLK STREET SCHOOL

THE BEAST IN MS. ROONEY'S ROOM
THE CANDY CORN CONTEST
LAZY LIONS, LUCKY LAMBS
IN THE DINOSAUR'S PAW
PURPLE CLIMBING DAYS *and more*

THE NEW KIDS AT THE POLK STREET SCHOOL

WATCH OUT! MAN-EATING SNAKE
FANCY FEET
ALL ABOUT STACY
B-E-S-T FRIENDS
SPECTACULAR STONE SOUP
STACY SAYS GOOD-BYE

YEARLING BOOKS/YOUNG YEARLINGS/YEARLING CLASSICS are designed especially to entertain and enlighten young people. Patricia Reilly Giff, consultant to this series, received her bachelor's degree from Marymount College and a master's degree in history from St. John's University. She holds a Professional Diploma in Reading and a Doctorate of Humane Letters from Hofstra University. She was a teacher and reading consultant for many years, and is the author of numerous books for young readers.

For a complete listing of all Yearling titles, write to
Dell Readers Service, P.O. Box 1045,
South Holland, IL 60473

YANKEE DOODLE DRUMSTICKS

Patricia Reilly Giff

Illustrated by
Emily Arnold McCully

A YOUNG YEARLING BOOK

Published by
DELL PUBLISHING
a division of
Bantam Doubleday Dell Publishing Group, Inc.
666 Fifth Avenue
New York, New York 10103

The trademark Yearling® is registered in the
U.S. Patent and Trademark Office.

The trademark Dell® is registered in the
U.S. Patent and Trademark Office.

ISBN 0-440-40518-1

Printed in the United States of America

October 1992

10 9 8 7 6 5 4 3 2 1

CWO

For William Langan Giff
—June 27, 1991—
Love and welcome!

♪ CHAPTER 1 ♪

Willie Roberts was humming.

It was a song his father liked to sing . . . something about Yankee Doodle going to London.

Willie loved to hum.

He loved the ticklish feeling in back of his nose.

He looked in the bathroom mirror.

He stopped humming.

He was a mess.

A filthy mess.

He splashed water over his face.

He slicked down his hair.

Then he went down the hall.

"Did you see my drumstick?" he asked his brother, Darrell.

Darrell poked his head out the bedroom door. "In the refrigerator."

Willie bent over. He tried to knot his sneaker lace.

The whole thing was gray and broken into pieces.

How was he going to be able to march . . . ? He looked up at Darrell. "What do you mean, the refrigerator?"

Darrell slapped his leg. "On the chicken. Get it? Drumstick?"

Willie wanted to give him a crack. That Darrell had such a fat mouth.

He didn't have time though. He had to find the drumstick and get over to the school.

"Take hold of yourself," Willie told Darrell as he went past.

He laughed a little. Mrs. Lovejoy, his teacher, said that about a million times a day.

Willie looked out the window on the stair landing.

It would be dark soon.

He hated the dark.

He had to get over to the school while he could still see . . . while he could watch out for robbers, and bad guys, and . . .

"Take hold of yourself," he whispered under his breath.

Tonight was the first practice night for the Lincoln Lions Band.

He had been waiting since school started.

He headed for the stairs.

He was dying to be a drummer.

For weeks he had been practicing with an old drumstick he had found.

He had practiced on the floor . . . on the walls . . . on top of the TV.

He loved the sound of it, even more than humming.

Nobody else in the house liked the sound.

He was driving Darrell crazy.

Too bad for Darrell.

Willie stepped around his little sister, Janell.

Janell was sitting on the bottom step.

She was bouncing her doll, Angelina, up and down.

It looked as if Angelina's head would bounce right off.

"Look, Willie," Janell said. "She's dancing."

Willie nodded. He took a quick look under the couch. Lots of things were under there, but no drumstick.

He spotted it under the dining room table.

He slid underneath, past his mother's legs.

She was barefoot, wiggling her toes, reading.

It was a book with numbers all over it. Things his mother taught up at the college.

"Your mother teaches people how to build bridges," his father had told him. "And I build them."

Willie yanked on his mother's toe a little.

He grabbed his drumstick. Then he backed out from under the table.

"Going to play the drums?" she asked. "You'll be spectacular."

"Parades," said Willie. "Contests. Going to be the best. Dad's going to come—"

"Don't start . . ."

"I've got to go. Right now," Willie said. "Right this minute."

He yanked at the sneaker lace. It broke off in his hand. "Now what am I going to do?"

"In the kitchen drawer," she said. "They're green though."

He banged into the kitchen. "Girl laces."

"Sale laces." She smiled at him. "Want me to walk you over?"

"You think I can't go three blocks by myself?" he asked. "You think I'm afraid?"

"Never," she said. "You're as strong as . . . as a . . . " She looked up at the ceiling.

"A lion," he finished for her. "A lion in the Lincoln Lions Band."

"Wear a sweater," his mother said.

"It's itchy," he said. "It's so itchy, I—"

His mother was taking a breath.

She'd be talking about sweaters and catching cold for the next hour.

"All right," he said. "All right."

He pulled the sweater over his head and slammed out the door.

It was darker than he thought. He wished

7

they had that daylight saving time thing back again.

It was colder too.

Three garbage cans stood in front of the house.

It would be easy for something to hide behind them. It could pop right out at him and . . .

He could see Kenny Bender heading down the street.

"Wait up," Willie shouted. He crashed across the leaves on the lawn.

He didn't look back at the garbage cans.

Kenny looked clean as a whistle.

Kenny always looked clean. He had a round, shiny kind of face.

Willie told himself he'd try to look good next time. He'd use a pile of soap on his face and hands.

He was going to be a great band kid.

He was going to practice up. Be a straight marcher.

There were going to be some big doings one of these days.

The professor said there was a surprise coming.

Willie figured they were going to march somewhere special on Thanksgiving.

He thought about his father.

Maybe his father would stop building bridges.

Maybe he'd come to see the band, and stay home forever.

Willie shook his head. He had asked his father to stay home before.

That day, his father had taken him in the car. They had driven a long way . . . just to see a bridge.

"See that," his father had said. "See how it curves up? See how straight the cables are? See the sun behind it?"

Willie had nodded. "Neat." He didn't want to hurt his father's feelings.

It was just an old gray bridge.

"I love that feeling," his father had said. "When I see one going up . . ."

Willie had nodded again. He was sleepy. He tried not to yawn.

For a moment his father had looked disappointed. Then he laughed. "Let's get some ice cream," he said. "Some peanut brittle fudge."

Right now Kenny was saying something . . . talking about how dark it was.

"Don't be a baby," he told Kenny. "There's nothing wrong with the dark."

He crossed his fingers.

Then he saw the big square lights of the school up ahead.

"Come on, Kenny," he said. "Let's not be the last ones in."

He began to hum. "Stuck a feather in his cap . . ."

He rushed through the schoolyard gates. "And called it macaroni."

♪ CHAPTER 2 ♪

Willie headed toward the gym ahead of Kenny.

Someone gave him a punch in the arm.

"Ouch." He whirled around.

It was his friend, Chrissie Tripp.

"Hey," she said, grinning. "It's band night."

He nodded at her, grinning back.

They turned in at the big gym doors.

The floor was shiny. It smelled a little like paint.

Chrissie's older sister, Teresa, was standing on the bleachers.

Teresa was the drum major. She was blowing a whistle as hard as she could. Her cheeks were all puffed out.

No one was paying any attention though. Kids were running all over the place.

He could see Ahmed and T.K. and Michelle sliding around.

"I hope I get to play a horn," said Kenny.

"Bugle, you mean," Chrissie said. "I'm going to be a fifer."

Willie didn't say anything.

He had seen a pile of fat round drums in the professor's music room.

Shiny drums.

He had even tried one with his drumstick.

It had the same ticklish sound as his humming.

He could feel it in his head and in his throat.

He could even feel it in his chest.

He wouldn't be Chrissie for anything . . . lips all puckered up like a lemon, tootling on a stick.

He wouldn't be Kenny with a bugle either.

Professor Thurman came through the door.

Sometimes they called him Professor Thum-de-dum.

He had gray hair.

It kind of whooshed around his head.

He had a mustache too.

It was gray and whooshy too.

He stood in the doorway for a minute.

One at a time, everyone stopped running.

It was quiet in the gym . . . quiet except for Teresa.

She blew the whistle twice more.

Then she saw the professor.

She clapped her hand over her mouth.

The professor scratched his head a little. "I think we'd better get into groups," he said. "Drummers near the bleachers. Buglers by the basketball hoop. Fifers in the middle."

Everyone started to run again.

They bumped into each other, laughing.

Teresa blew her whistle again.

The professor raised one hand. "Easy," he said.

Willie took it easy. He didn't want to get into trouble the first night.

He passed Chrissie in the fife group.

It didn't look as if there were many fifers. Just a couple of girls.

"We need some fifers," the professor was saying.

Willie hid behind a big kid in the drum section.

He didn't want the professor to pick him out.

The last thing he wanted to be was a fifer. He had to be a drummer.

The big kid slid in behind someone else. The professor looked straight at Willie. Willie held up his drumstick.

He was glad he had one.

The professor smiled. He looked toward some other kids.

Willie bent over.

He tapped his drumstick on the floor. Rat-a-tat tat.

Terrific.

The big kid in front of him turned around. "Lay off," he said.

Willie stood up.

The kid was too big to fool around with.

He made believe he didn't hear him. He looked out the window until the kid moved away. It was dark outside now.

Very dark.

Take hold, Willie, he told himself.

He slid over next to Kenny Bender and tapped him on the head with the drumstick.

♪ CHAPTER 3 ♪

The next day, Willie slid down the hall.

He stopped at Room 201.

Mrs. Lovejoy had pasted a red-and-brown turkey on the door.

Willie banged on its tail. Pom-pom pom-pom.

The pomming sounded like a drum ruff.

He had learned ruffs last night at band practice.

He opened the door and went inside.

Mrs. Lovejoy was up at the board, writing a bunch of spelling words.

She looked over her shoulder. "Is that you drumming, Willie?" She was frowning.

"Sorry." Willie marched to the closet. He made a sharp right turn. Right heel down, left heel up. Swing your feet. Bang them together.

Terrific.

Just the way he learned it at the Lincoln Lions Band.

"Great right turn," T. K. Meaney said from inside the closet.

Willie nodded. He yanked his sweater over his head.

He rolled it into a ball and threw it at T.K.

T.K. grabbed someone's jacket.

He tossed it over Willie's head.

"I am in a tomb," Willie said.

"You'd better be in your seat," called Mrs. Lovejoy.

Willie threw the jacket back on a hook.

He followed T.K. to their seats.

He had a new seat this week. A seat in front.

Mrs. Lovejoy said he was doing too much fooling around in back.

Usually he hated to sit in front.

But this time it wasn't so bad. T.K. was on one side.

Chrissie Tripp was on the other side.

Right now she was making eraser pictures on her desk.

The whole thing was a mess.

She looked up. "News," she told him.

Willie leaned over.

From the other side, T.K. leaned over too.

Chrissie stared at T.K. "Private news."

T.K. sat back.

Willie could tell he was listening though.

Chrissie squinted her eyes at T.K. "I'll put it in a note," she told Willie.

She pulled out a piece of paper.

At the same time, Mrs. Lovejoy turned to the class.

She tapped on the board with her chalk.

Willie pulled his shoulders together.

Mrs. Lovejoy loved to make the chalk screech.

This time it sounded like a drum ruff. Click-click click-click.

"Make up sentences," said Mrs. Lovejoy. "One for every word."

Willie tried to pull his notebook out of his desk.

Everything else came with it.

His health book. A bunch of old pencils. His speller.

"Get it together," Mrs. Lovejoy said.

Willie bent over to pick everything up.

Then he sat up high.

He tried to see what Chrissie was writing.

Chrissie was left-handed. Her arm covered the note.

He opened his notebook.

The cover was coming off.

There were about three pages left.

He had played Hangman on most of the others.

He hoped Mrs. Lovejoy wouldn't see.

Chrissie tossed the note on his desk.

> TERESA TOLE JESSICA.
>
> WE'RE GETTING UNIFORMS.
>
> WE'RE PLAYING AT A FUTBALL GAME
>
> ON THANKSGIVING.

Willie looked across at her. "Really?"

Chrissie nodded. "My sister's president of the school, isn't she? Drum major too."

"How many sentences do you have finished?" Mrs. Lovejoy asked Chrissie.

"One and a half," Chrissie said.

"And you, Willie?"

"I'm doing my heading," Willie said.

He picked up his pencil.

He looked up at the first word on the blackboard.

Love.

Mrs. Lovejoy liked to stick things in about herself sometimes.

Last week they had had *joy*.

Willie stared at his paper.

He thought about *love*.

His father had told him that the *l*'s in his name meant love.

Darrell had *l*'s too.

So did Janell.

His father and mother had named them that way on purpose.

Willie would never tell anyone that. It was too embarrassing.

It made Willie feel good though.

He smoothed out his paper.

Love, he wrote. *I love cheken soop.*

His father loved football.

Then he thought of something. Something terrific.

Willie half closed his eyes. It looked as if his writing was all scrunched up on the paper.

He was thinking of himself in a shiny red-and-blue uniform.

He'd be out on the football field.

He'd be drumming away.

And his father would be there.

This would be a terrific Thanksgiving.

Willie couldn't remember when his father had been home for Thanksgiving last.

If only his father would come.

♪ CHAPTER 4 ♩

On Thursday night, Willie sat on the bathroom floor.

He had two drumsticks now. The professor had given them to him at practice.

First he played them on the edge of the tub.

Then he tried the pipes under the sink.

They made a terrific sound.

Janell popped her head in the door. "You're giving Angelina a headache," she said.

"One more minute," he said. He wanted to hear them on the faucets.

"Just one," said Janell.

Willie nodded. He swished the drumsticks against the floor.

They sounded whispery . . . neat.

Darrell pounded down the hall. "Are you out of your mind?"

Willie tried to close the door. He tried to get it locked before Darrell could get in.

"Oof." Darrell's foot caught in the edge.

Willie tried to push it back with his own foot.

"If I get hold of you, Willie," Darrell yelled, "I'm going to bash your head—"

Their mother came up the stairs. "Into your room," she told Darrell. "Out of the bathroom," she told Willie.

Darrell looked back over his shoulder. "I win," he said.

"You may win a week without television," said their mother.

"I have to do something anyway," said Willie.

He went down to his bedroom and looked around for his notebook. It was on the windowsill.

He tore a piece out of the back.

Mrs. Lovejoy would have a fit if she knew.

He pulled out the edges that were left in the book.

Next he needed a pencil. A decent one.

"Janell?" he called. He went down to her room.

She had last summer's beach shells in rows on the floor. "Which one is the best?" she asked.

"I don't know. They all look the same," he said. "How about lending me a pencil?"

She looked up. Her forehead crinkled. "I have only two nice pointy ones."

Willie sighed. "Come on, Janell. This is important."

"Why?"

He leaned forward. "I'm writing to Dad. I'm telling him to come home for Thanksgiving."

Janell shook her head a little. "He's too far."

"Will you just lend me the pencil? Just stop talking and . . ."

She got up from the floor, stepped between her shells, and opened her dresser drawer.

Janell was the neatest kid in the world. She pulled out her pencil box.

"Make believe you don't know it's here," she said. "I don't want you taking all my stuff."

Willie grinned. He grabbed the pencil. He raced down to the basement.

It was dark down there, but not the scary kind.

He turned on the light in his father's workroom.

It wasn't a real workroom.

His father never used it.

Willie used it though. He had a million things in there. Old comics, pieces of wood, a bunch of LEGOs.

He sat on the floor, leaning the paper against the wall.

Then he began to write.

Dear Dad,

    I am in a band. Me and Chrissy Tripp.

    I am a drummer.

    We are having the greatst unfarms. Red and bloo.

    Plese come hom for a Thankgiving thing. We are going to play.

    You will love it.

                 Your son,
            William T. Roberts

Willie sat back. He shook his hand back and forth.

It hurt from all that writing.

The letter was a little messy, because the wall wasn't even.

You could see the bumps on the paper. So what?

He could hear his mother coming down the stairs.

She was coming slowly.

She probably had a huge basket of wash.

He thought about reading her his letter. Maybe not.

She'd start telling him that his father might not be able to come.

No. He'd wait for his father to get there.

It would be a great surprise.

♪ CHAPTER 5 ♪

It was Saturday morning. They had just finished band practice.

"Junior band practice," Chrissie said.

She didn't have to remind him.

Willie knew very well they were just juniors.

Hadn't his Thanksgiving plan just been ruined?

There wouldn't be any uniforms for juniors.

They were just going to march along behind the seniors.

They were going to wear any old junk.

"Stop." Chrissie held her arms out on
each side. "Don't move. I just thought of
something."

Willie took one more step.

Chrissie was bossy.

The bossiest thing he had ever met.

She always had great ideas though.

"The only reason we're not getting uniforms is because of money."

"So?"

"We'll get it ourselves," Chrissie said.

Willie nodded slowly. They'd earn a pile
of money, turn it right over to the professor
and . . .

"How?" he asked.

"How?" Chrissie repeated. "Simple. We'll
sell something."

She looked up at the sky. "Pretzels. We'll

buy a box at ShopRite. We'll split it open and sell it up at the college."

She looked back at him. Her blue eyes crinkled up. "Drop your drumsticks off, and your drum pad. Don't go wasting a hundred minutes on junk."

Willie opened his mouth. Then he closed it again.

"Hurry," she said. "Thanksgiving is coming fast."

He turned up his driveway and went into the house. She was right about Thanksgiving. His mother had a bunch of strange-looking nuts in a bowl. They were always there for Thanksgiving, but no one ate them. She always threw them out the next day.

He dropped his drum pad in the hall, and stuck his drumsticks in his back pockets.

They stuck out a mile.

Good.

It would be great for all those college people to know he was a drummer.

He wished there was time to go to the bathroom . . . to get a drink . . . to find something to eat.

But Chrissie would be mad as anything if she had to wait.

He thought back to practice this morning.

He had learned all about paradiddles. Drum with the right hand, the left hand, the right hand, right. Then left hand, right hand, left hand, left.

Terrific.

Poor old bossy Chrissie.

All she had learned was how to make a couple of notes on the fife.

He banged out the front door again, crossed the lawn.

Leaves were piled up all over the place.

He shuffled through them.

He and Chrissie had to sell thousands of pretzels.

Willie closed his eyes for a minute.

He was banging a drum in the middle of the football field.

He hummed a little "Yankee Doodle."

The red-and-blue uniforms flashed by.

The crowd couldn't believe it.

"Terrific," someone yelled.

Everyone began to clap . . . to roar.

His father, mother, Janell, and even Darrell were little specks in the fourteenth row.

His father was cheering as loud as he could.

"That's right," said Chrissie. "Knock yourself out on a telephone pole. Only an idiot would walk along with his eyes closed."

Willie opened his eyes. "Hey," he said. "I just thought of something. Where are we going to get the money to buy all these pretzels?"

Chrissie looked impatient. "I knew you'd say that."

She reached into her pocket. "I have all my birthday money. And you . . ."

Willie bit his lip. "I'm saving . . ."

"You have money," Chrissie said. "You have exactly . . ."

He could feel the teeth marks on his lower lip.

Chrissie knew everything. She was so nosy, she didn't miss anything.

"I'm saving it to visit my father," he said. "You know that."

Then he stopped.

He'd have to put that visiting business off for a while. His father was coming home anyway.

"I'll owe you," he said. "I'll give it to you tomorrow."

"Fifty-fifty," she said, holding out her hand.

He slapped hers. "All right."

He felt in his pocket.

The letter was there.

"I have to stop at the post office," he told Chrissie.

She rolled her eyes. "We have to go to ShopRite."

"It'll just take two minutes," he said. "You don't have to get all excited just for—"

She gritted her teeth. "Then hurry, will you?"

Willie turned the corner. He hurried to the door of the post office.

He was sick of hurrying.

He looked at the two bins. IN TOWN. OUT OF TOWN.

He wanted OUT.

He tipped the envelope in.

He wished it were a little cleaner.

Then he dashed outside to catch up with Chrissie.

♪ CHAPTER 6 ♪

Willie and Chrissie dragged her mother's table up the college walk.

Willie was doing paradiddles in his head.

"Stop eating those pretzels," she told him.

"I'm just taking a little salt," he said.

The campus was crowded.

They had to wait forever to cross the penny bridge.

"Why don't we just set up here?" Willie asked.

"Dumb bridge," Chrissie said. "Takes so long." She looked at him. "You want to get the most people, don't you? Look at everyone sitting over there on the grass." She frowned at him. "Stop eating."

"I am," he said.

They crossed the bridge and set up the table.

Three girls swooped over. "Pretzels?" one asked. "Great idea."

"This one's a little wet," said another one.

Chrissie glared at Willie.

He took out his drumsticks. "We're saving for uniforms," he said.

The girl put a quarter on the table. "For a band? Can you play the drums?"

Willie did a couple of quick ruffs on the table.

Then he did a paradiddle.

"Wow," said the first girl. "What about you?" she asked Chrissie.

"Fife." Chrissie raised one shoulder. "It's home." She started to straighten the pretzels.

"Hey, Eddie," the girl yelled across the lawn. "These kids are saving for uniforms."

Willie and Chrissie nodded at each other.

"We're coming up here on Thanksgiving," said Chrissie. "Going to play at the football game."

Eddie bought a pretzel too. "You have to sell a lot of these to make any money . . ."

He broke off. "How come this one doesn't have any salt?"

"Sorry," Willie said. "I just took a . . ."

Eddie put the pretzel back on the table. He wiped his hands on his jeans.

"Good luck," he said. "I'll look for you on Thanksgiving."

"Me too," said one of the girls.

They all went down the path.

"Is that rain?" Willie asked.

Chrissie held her hand out. "No."

"People are leaving," said Willie.

"It's not rain," said Chrissie.

"I wish it would snow," said Willie.

He watched people hurrying up the path, away from them.

"Nice fresh pretzels," Chrissie yelled after someone.

"What time do you think it is?" Willie asked.

He broke the edge off a pretzel and stuck it in his mouth.

"Willie!" Chrissie said.

He made believe he wasn't chewing.

It was cold now, and windy. If it weren't for those uniforms . . . if it weren't for his father, he'd forget about this whole thing.

He could see his father coming home. He'd come in the yellow pickup truck, up the driveway. Just like last time.

They hadn't known he was coming.

Everyone was eating stuffed shells in the living room.

The whole place was a mess.

His mother had her books spread out on the floor.

Darrell was building something, something with a lot of wood, and Willie was . . .

He couldn't even remember what he had been doing.

His father had stood in the doorway, laughing.

Willie sighed. The trouble was, his father had only stayed two weeks that time.

He was always going somewhere, building another bridge.

"Wake up," Chrissie said. "Someone's going to come any minute."

Willie looked down the path. "Everyone's gone."

"It's your fault," Chrissie said. "Getting those pretzels all wet."

Her lip stuck out past her chin.

Willie felt a drop of rain, and then another.

He shivered.

Chrissie kept talking and talking. Her hands were on her hips now.

Without thinking, he took another bit of salt from a pretzel.

"There," Chrissie said. "See what I mean?"

"I'm going home," he said.

"You can't leave me with all these pretzels," Chrissie said. "Wet with all the salt gone."

Willie kicked at the table leg. "My father's coming home soon. I'm going to get ready."

"Your father isn't coming home," Chrissie said. "That's a big lie."

"You don't know," he said. "You don't know one thing about it."

He started across the bridge.

A car horn blared behind him.

Willie didn't even look back.

"Never mind," he told himself. That's what his mother always said.

He passed the post office.

He wondered where his letter was.

Maybe by this time it would be on a plane to California. On the way to his father.

He shook his head.

Chrissie was right. His father would never come. And if he did, he'd see Willie looking silly without a uniform in the Lincoln Lions Band.

♪ CHAPTER 7 ♪

Willie opened his eyes as wide as he could.

He tried not to blink.

It was so black in his bedroom, anyone could be standing in the corner.

It was all because of Darrell.

Darrell had turned the hall light out on purpose.

Willie thought about getting up.

He thought about turning the light on again.

Darrell would laugh.

He hated Darrell sometimes.

He turned over so he could look out the window. It was dark out there too.

Take hold, he told himself.

His father told him that most kids were afraid of the dark. He said it just went away by itself.

Willie took a quick look at his dresser. It was a big dark block in the corner.

Every cent in his top drawer belonged to Chrissie for those pretzels.

He wondered what had happened with them.

He took a breath.

A pounding noise was coming down the hall.

He ducked under the blanket.

Then he realized it was Janell.

She dived on the edge of the bed.

"There's noise all over the place," she said. "Someone's coming."

"Don't be silly," Darrell said from the other bed.

Willie didn't say anything.

"Willie?" Janell asked.

"It's all right," he said.

She yanked the bottom of the blanket up to cover her feet. "I guess I'll stay awhile."

"Babies," Darrell said.

Willie felt around for a book on the night table.

He threw it as hard as he could toward Darrell's bed.

It hit the wall.

"Try that again and I'll cream you," Darrell said.

"Don't pay attention," Janell said. "Talk to me, Willie."

Willie took a deep breath.

When his father came home, he was going to ask for karate lessons.

And when he did . . . when he got his black belt, Darrell would be out of luck.

"I told Daddy you were going to be a drummer," Janell said.

Willie sat up a little.

His eyes were getting used to the dark.

He could see Janell sitting on the end of the bed.

She was chewing on the end of her long, dark hair.

"How did you tell Daddy that?" he asked slowly.

"A red uniform, shiny, just like you said," Janell said. "With a great big drum. Pounding and pounding."

She pulled the blanket a little harder. "What do you call that?"

"A ruff?" Willie asked.

"Yes. Pom-pom pom-pom." Her voice was getting sleepy.

"What about Daddy?" Willie asked.

"He's going to build a bridge . . . a wide

bridge . . . I think it's a money bridge," she said. "Something like that."

In the other bed, Darrell sat up. "When did you talk to him?"

"Today," said Janell.

"You didn't tell anyone."

"I'm telling Willie," Janell said. "Right now."

"Is he coming home?" Willie asked.

His mouth was dry. He could see his father coming in the back door, laughing.

He could see his mother sitting at the dining room table, looking up.

Then he saw himself, wearing his green shirt.

He was marching down the field, looking silly. He was following all the senior band kids.

His father was in the fourteenth row with his mother and Janell.

Darrell was there, too, laughing.

But Darrell wasn't laughing now.

Willie was surprised.

Darrell was asking Janell, "Is he coming?" His voice sounded excited.

Darrell didn't sound as tough as he usually did.

Willie swallowed.

Janell sucked on her hair again. "I don't know," she said.

♪ CHAPTER 8 ♩

It was Wednesday, the last day of school before Thanksgiving.

Willie walked out of the classroom.

The hall was empty.

He ran the eraser end of his pencil along the bricks . . . up and down . . . like ocean waves.

Too bad he wasn't at the ocean.

Too bad he had to go back to his classroom in about two and a half minutes.

He headed for the water fountain.

56

He'd been in trouble since he had gotten to school that morning.

One . . . he was late. The band had practiced and practiced last night. He couldn't get himself going this morning.

Two . . . he had forgotten his book report.

Three . . . Chrissie kept telling him she wanted the pretzel money.

Four . . .

"Willie," a man's voice called.

Willie turned.

The professor was coming in the door.

He was balancing boxes and bags and a long black cello case.

"Need some help?" Willie asked.

"Great. Terrific," said the professor. He sounded out of breath.

They walked downstairs to the music room. Willie carried a couple of bags that smelled like pickles and cheese.

He carried the cello case too.

It probably weighed as much as the professor, Willie thought.

"Too heavy?" the professor asked.

"Nah," said Willie. "Light as a feather."

They started down the stairs.

Willie went as fast as he could.

If they didn't get to the music room soon, he'd drop everything. Pickles, cheese, and cello case.

The professor would think he was an idiot.

"I'm late," said the professor. "I give cello lessons at the college. The traffic on the bridge was . . ."

He stopped for a breath. "Terrible. I'll be glad when they get to work on it."

Willie thought back to the other day.

The pretzel day.

He didn't like to think about it.

He shouldn't have eaten the salt off them.

He shouldn't have . . .

The professor rubbed at his mustache. "Eddie was asking about you. That was another reason I was late."

"Eddie?" Willie looked up. He tried to shift the cello case.

It felt as if his fingers were crushed.

So what if the professor was late, he thought.

Mrs. Lovejoy couldn't do one thing about that.

"Good student, that Eddie," said the professor.

He put down his packages.

He reached into his pocket. "The key is here somewhere."

Willie set the cello case on the floor.

He had no feeling in his fingers.

"Do you like cheese?" the professor asked.

"Uh . . ." Willie said. "I don't think . . ."

The professor smiled. "My favorite food. No matter."

He turned the key in the lock and opened the music room door.

An odd smell drifted out of the room.

More cheese, Willie thought.

The professor looked down at him. "I'll tell you one thing," he said. "That cello case is pretty heavy. I'll tell you something else."

The professor leaned forward. "You're a good drummer. You're going to be great someday."

Willie opened his mouth.

Great someday.

He couldn't believe it.

"I can only ruff," Willie said. "And paradiddle."

The professor shook his head. "You've got music in you," he said. "I know."

Willie put his hand up to his mouth. His lips felt strange.

The professor smiled. "You know it, don't you? You know I'm right."

A warm feeling was spreading in Willie's chest.

It was so big, he could hardly breathe.

He nodded.

Then he backed out of the room.

Great someday.

He remembered his father saying something once. "Someday I'm going to build a great bridge."

Willie went up the stairs.

He had to do his book report.

He had to take his money out of his coat and give it to Chrissie.

He thought about his father again.

Maybe his father felt about bridges the way he did about drumming.

♪ CHAPTER 9 ♩

It was Thanksgiving morning.

Everyone was racing around the gym, sliding on the floors.

Teresa was blowing her whistle.

Willie took a couple of cracks on the head from Kenny Bender's bugle.

Chrissie was hopping up and down.

They were friends again.

She hadn't even taken all his money . . . only half.

He was starting to save up to visit his father again.

He wondered where he'd be.

"Into places," Teresa screamed.

Willie stopped to pick up his drum.

He bent his head to fasten the straps over his shoulders.

Then he headed toward the back row.

He tried a quick ruff.

It sounded terrific.

The professor came into the gym. He was carrying a pile of wide blue ribbons.

He waved them in the air.

"These are for the junior band," he said. "To wear over their shoulders."

The professor put one over his own shoulder. He tucked it into his belt.

LINCOLN LIONS was written in gold letters across the front.

"From some people at the college," said the professor. "They wanted to help out."

Chrissie looked back at Willie.

They both smiled.

The college people were the girls and Eddie. They both knew that.

Willie waited for Teresa to pass out the ribbons.

They looked spectacular . . . almost as good as having uniforms.

Then they were ready to go.

"Forrrrr-waarrrd march," yelled Teresa.

The band began to move.

Up in front Willie could see T.K. Meaney carrying the flag, and Jessica Martinez, the leader of the juniors.

They took a sharp right turn out the door.

Outside, everything felt crisp.

There had been some frost last night.

"Left-two-three-four," Teresa shouted.

The lead drummer began to drum. Pom. Pom. Pom.

Willie could feel it in time with his feet.

The professor was marching at the end of the line. He smiled at Willie.

They turned, and turned again.

Then it was time to cross the bridge.

It was lined with cars.

The traffic was stopped.

Teresa blew her whistle. "Mark time . . . march."

Willie lifted his feet, up and down, in place.

He felt good, he felt wonderful.

If only his father were there.

Teresa waved her baton. "Halt," she screamed.

Willie stopped drumming.

He could still hear the pounding in his head.

He could hear something else too. The professor was mumbling under his breath.

"That bridge," he said. "It's a good thing they're going to build a new one. No more penny bridge. It'll be a dollar one."

Then, suddenly, the traffic began to move.

Teresa blew her whistle.

The drums started up.

Then the bugles.

You could almost hear the fifes.

The band started across the bridge.

Willie could see everyone on the other side, waiting for them, waiting for the football game to begin.

Pom. Pom.

Build a new bridge.

Willie could hear it, could feel it.

They were in the park now.

In a minute, they'd be heading for the football field.

Everyone would be there. His mother, and Janell in a new dress.

Even Darrell had said he was coming.

Willie rolled the sticks across the drum.

Build a bridge.

Someone was going to build a new bridge.

A money bridge.

He knew who it was. Janell had said it.

He knew his father was going to be in the stands with the rest of the family.

His father probably wouldn't be home for that long.

Long enough to build that bridge though.

Willie was going to tell him about drumming, and music. Maybe they'd go down to look at the bridge together.

"To the right flank, march," Teresa screamed.

Willie took a breath.

He drummed as hard as he could.

The band turned onto the football field.

He looked up.

Everyone was there, just the way he had pictured it. Everyone was waving.

His father was smiling.

Willie started to smile too.

He raised one stick. Then he began to drum again.